My Little Pony: Friends Forever

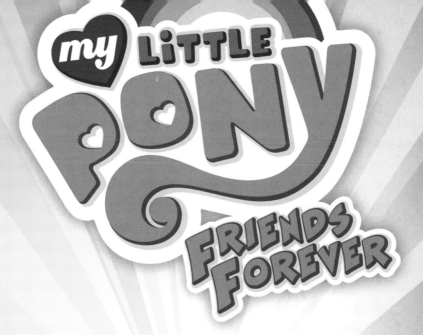

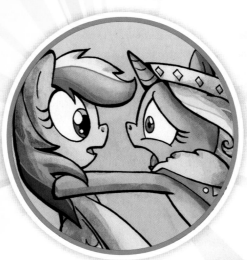

Rainbow Dash & Trixie

Written by
Thom Zahler

Art by
Agnes Garbowska

Lettered by
Neil Uyetake

ABDO Spotlight

IDW

ABDOPUBLISHING.COM

Reinforced library bound edition published in 2017 by Spotlight,
a division of ABDO, PO Box 398166, Minneapolis, Minnesota 55439.
Spotlight produces high-quality reinforced library bound editions for
schools and libraries. Published by agreement with IDW.

Printed in the United States of America, North Mankato, Minnesota.
042016
092016

THIS BOOK CONTAINS
RECYCLED MATERIALS

Licensed By:

LIBRARY OF CONGRESS CATALOGING-IN-PUBLICATION DATA

Names: Zahler, Thomas F., author. | Garbowska, Agnes, illustrator.
Title: Rainbow Dash & Trixie / writer, Thom Zahler ; art, Agnes Garbowska ;
    letters, Neil Uyetake.
Description: Reinforced library bound edition. | Minneapolis, Minnesota :
    Spotlight, 2017. | Series: My little pony: friends forever
Identifiers: LCCN 2016000303 | ISBN 9781614795117
Subjects: LCSH: Graphic novels.
Classification: LCC PZ7.7.Z35 Rai 2016 | DDC 741.5/973--dc23
LC record available at https://lccn.loc.gov/2016000303

Spotlight

A Division of ABDO
abdopublishing.com

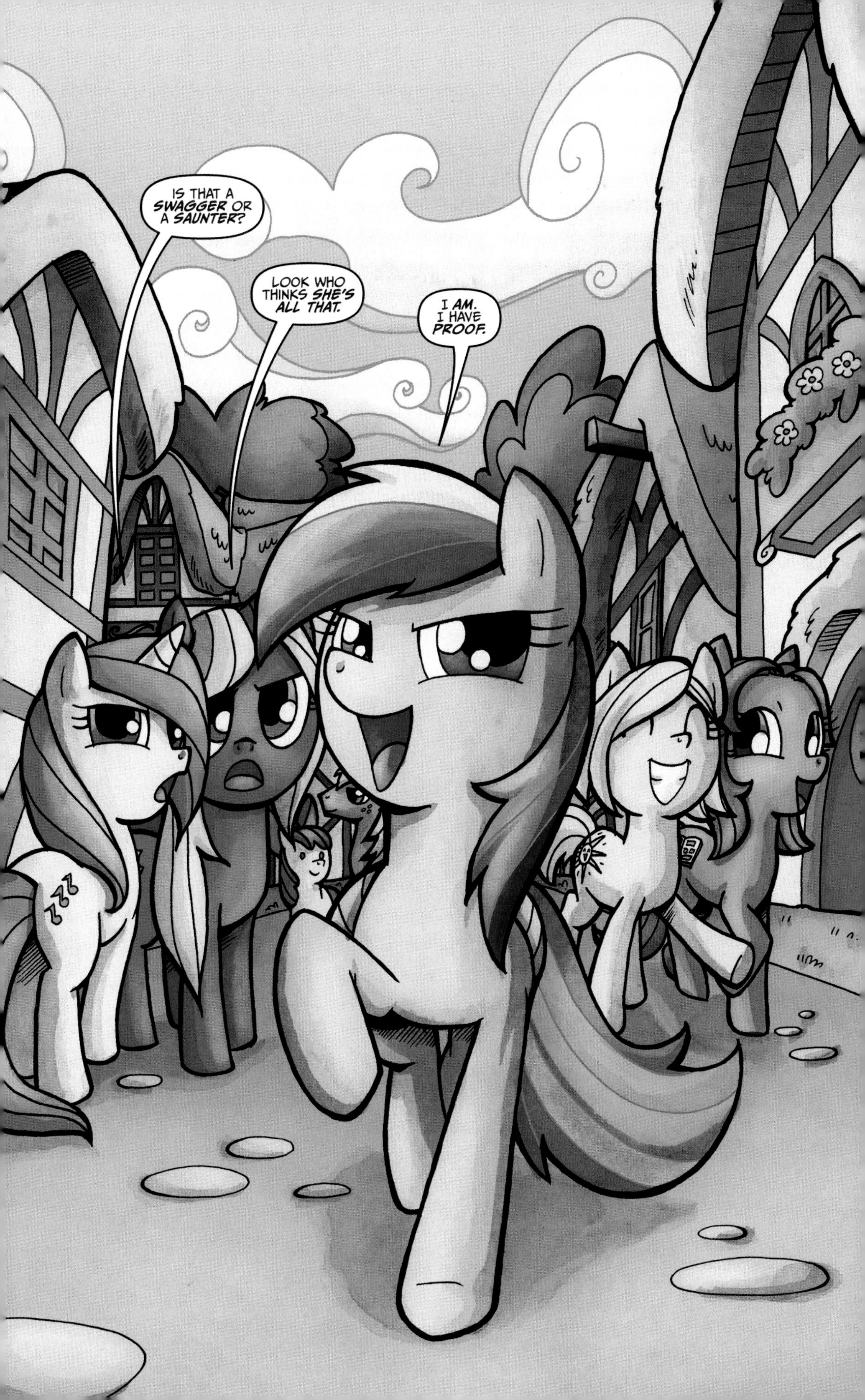
IS THAT A SWAGGER OR A SAUNTER?
LOOK WHO THINKS SHE'S ALL THAT.
I AM. I HAVE PROOF.

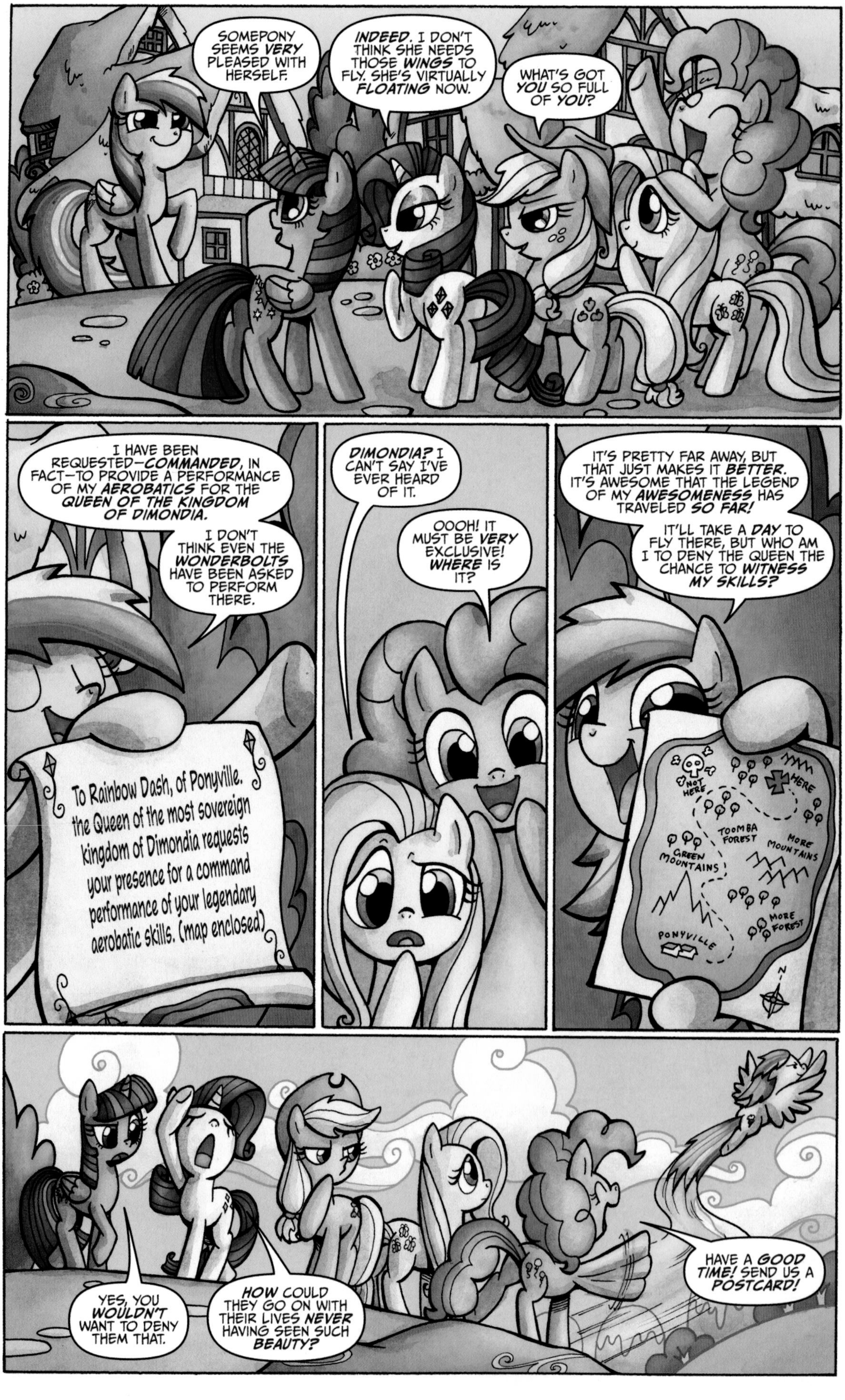
SOMEPONY SEEMS VERY PLEASED WITH HERSELF.
INDEED. I DON'T THINK SHE NEEDS THOSE WINGS TO FLY. SHE'S VIRTUALLY FLOATING NOW.
WHAT'S GOT YOU SO FULL OF YOU?
I HAVE BEEN REQUESTED—COMMANDED, IN FACT—TO PROVIDE A PERFORMANCE OF MY AEROBATICS FOR THE QUEEN OF THE KINGDOM OF DIMONDIA.
I DON'T THINK EVEN THE WONDERBOLTS HAVE BEEN ASKED TO PERFORM THERE.
To Rainbow Dash, of Ponyville. the Queen of the most sovereign kingdom of Dimondia requests your presence for a command performance of your legendary aerobatic skills. (map enclosed)
DIMONDIA? I CAN'T SAY I'VE EVER HEARD OF IT.
OOOH! IT MUST BE VERY EXCLUSIVE! WHERE IS IT?
IT'S PRETTY FAR AWAY, BUT THAT JUST MAKES IT BETTER. IT'S AWESOME THAT THE LEGEND OF MY AWESOMENESS HAS TRAVELED SO FAR!
IT'LL TAKE A DAY TO FLY THERE, BUT WHO AM I TO DENY THE QUEEN THE CHANCE TO WITNESS MY SKILLS?
NOT HERE
HERE
TOOMBA FOREST
MORE MOUNTAINS
GREEN MOUNTAINS
MORE FOREST
PONYVILLE
N
YES, YOU WOULDN'T WANT TO DENY THEM THAT.
HOW COULD THEY GO ON WITH THEIR LIVES NEVER HAVING SEEN SUCH BEAUTY?
HAVE A GOOD TIME! SEND US A POSTCARD!

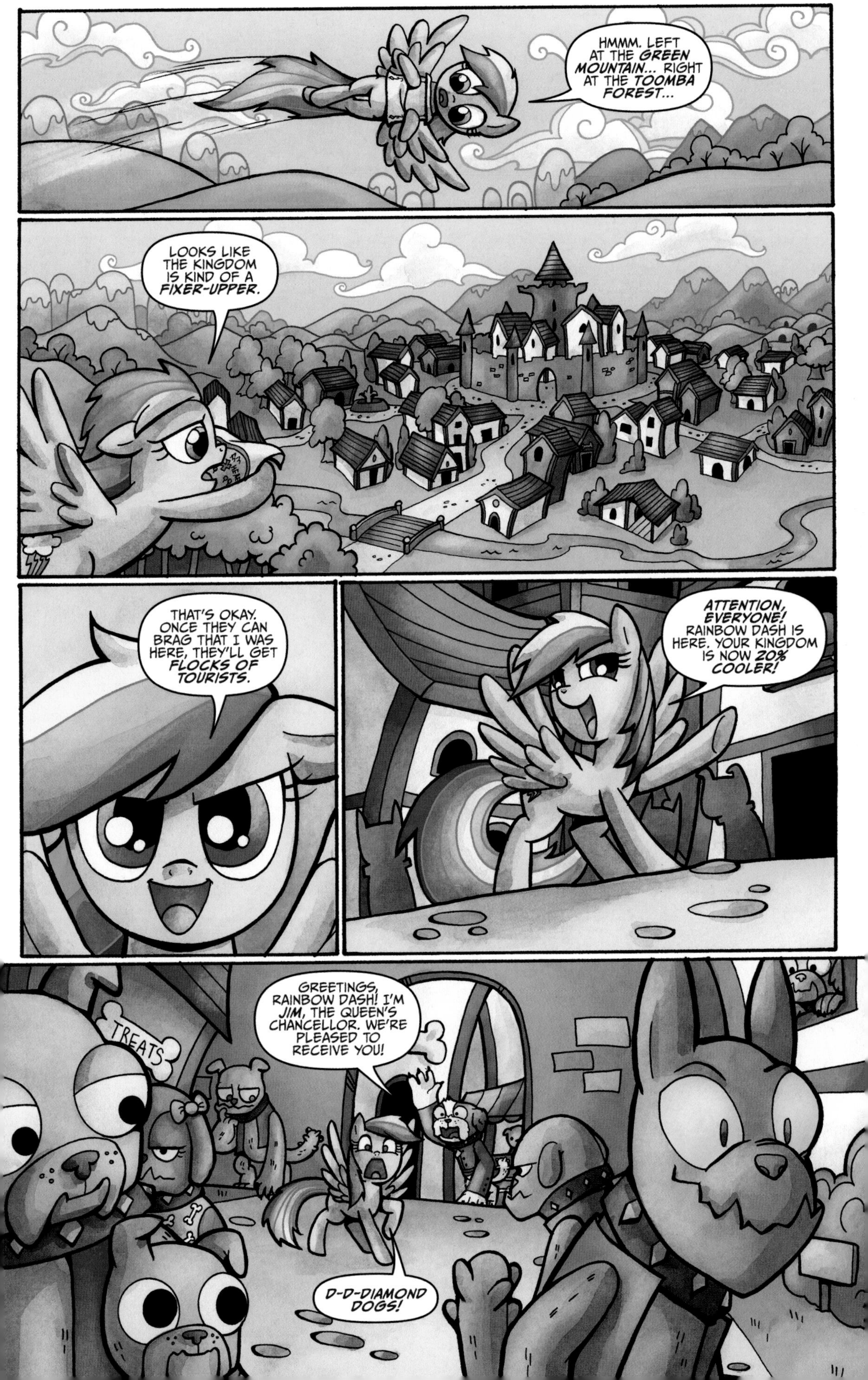
HMMM. LEFT AT THE GREEN MOUNTAIN... RIGHT AT THE TOOMBA FOREST...
LOOKS LIKE THE KINGDOM IS KIND OF A FIXER-UPPER.
THAT'S OKAY. ONCE THEY CAN BRAG THAT I WAS HERE, THEY'LL GET FLOCKS OF TOURISTS.
ATTENTION, EVERYONE! RAINBOW DASH IS HERE. YOUR KINGDOM IS NOW 20% COOLER!
TREATS
GREETINGS, RAINBOW DASH! I'M JIM, THE QUEEN'S CHANCELLOR. WE'RE PLEASED TO RECEIVE YOU!
D-D-DIAMOND DOGS!

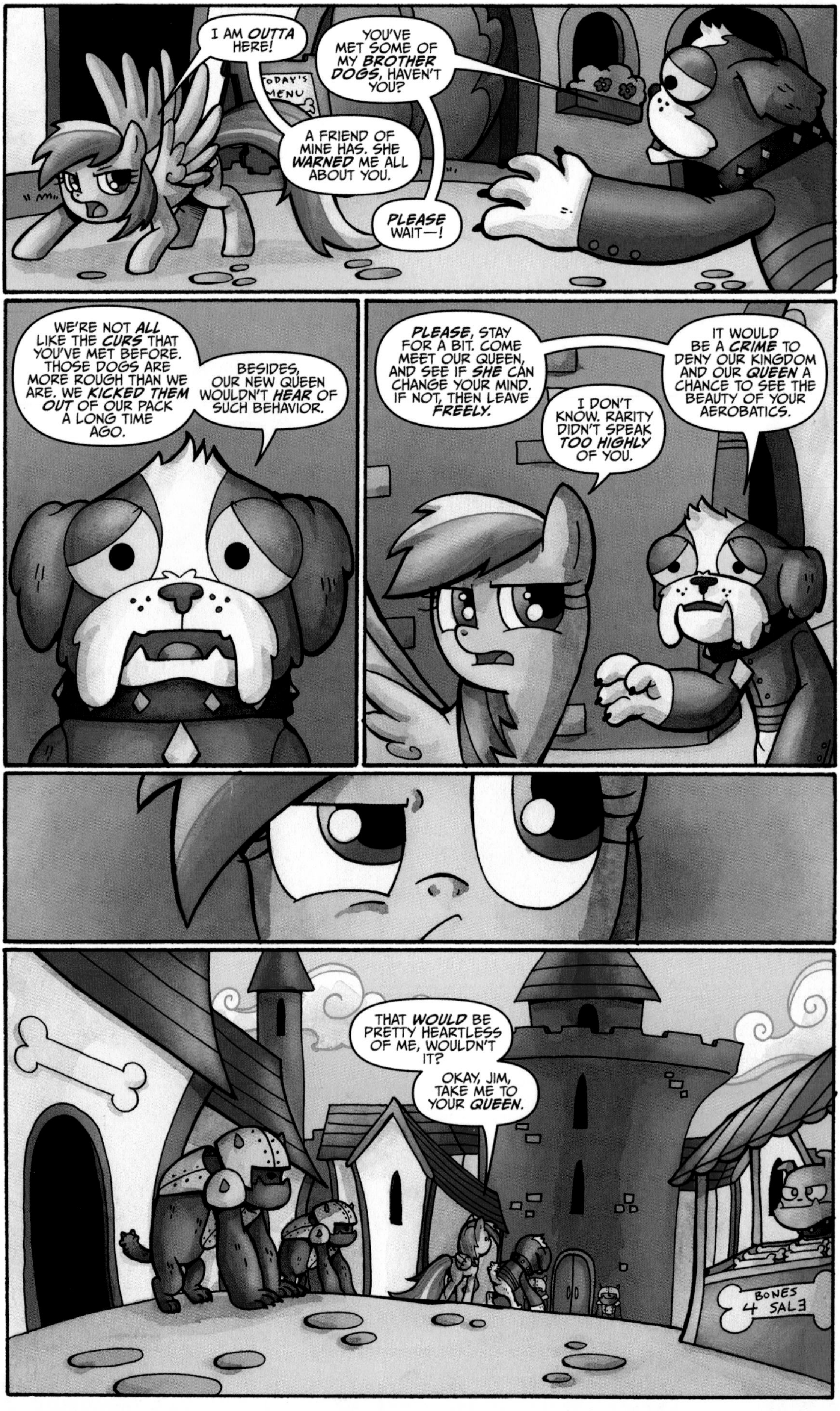
I AM OUTTA HERE!
YOU'VE MET SOME OF MY BROTHER DOGS, HAVEN'T YOU?
TODAY'S MENU
A FRIEND OF MINE HAS. SHE WARNED ME ALL ABOUT YOU.
PLEASE WAIT—!
WE'RE NOT ALL LIKE THE CURS THAT YOU'VE MET BEFORE. THOSE DOGS ARE MORE ROUGH THAN WE ARE. WE KICKED THEM OUT OF OUR PACK A LONG TIME AGO.
BESIDES, OUR NEW QUEEN WOULDN'T HEAR OF SUCH BEHAVIOR.
PLEASE, STAY FOR A BIT. COME MEET OUR QUEEN, AND SEE IF SHE CAN CHANGE YOUR MIND. IF NOT, THEN LEAVE FREELY.
IT WOULD BE A CRIME TO DENY OUR KINGDOM AND OUR QUEEN A CHANCE TO SEE THE BEAUTY OF YOUR AEROBATICS.
I DON'T KNOW. RARITY DIDN'T SPEAK TOO HIGHLY OF YOU.
THAT WOULD BE PRETTY HEARTLESS OF ME, WOULDN'T IT?
OKAY, JIM, TAKE ME TO YOUR QUEEN.
BONES 4 SALE

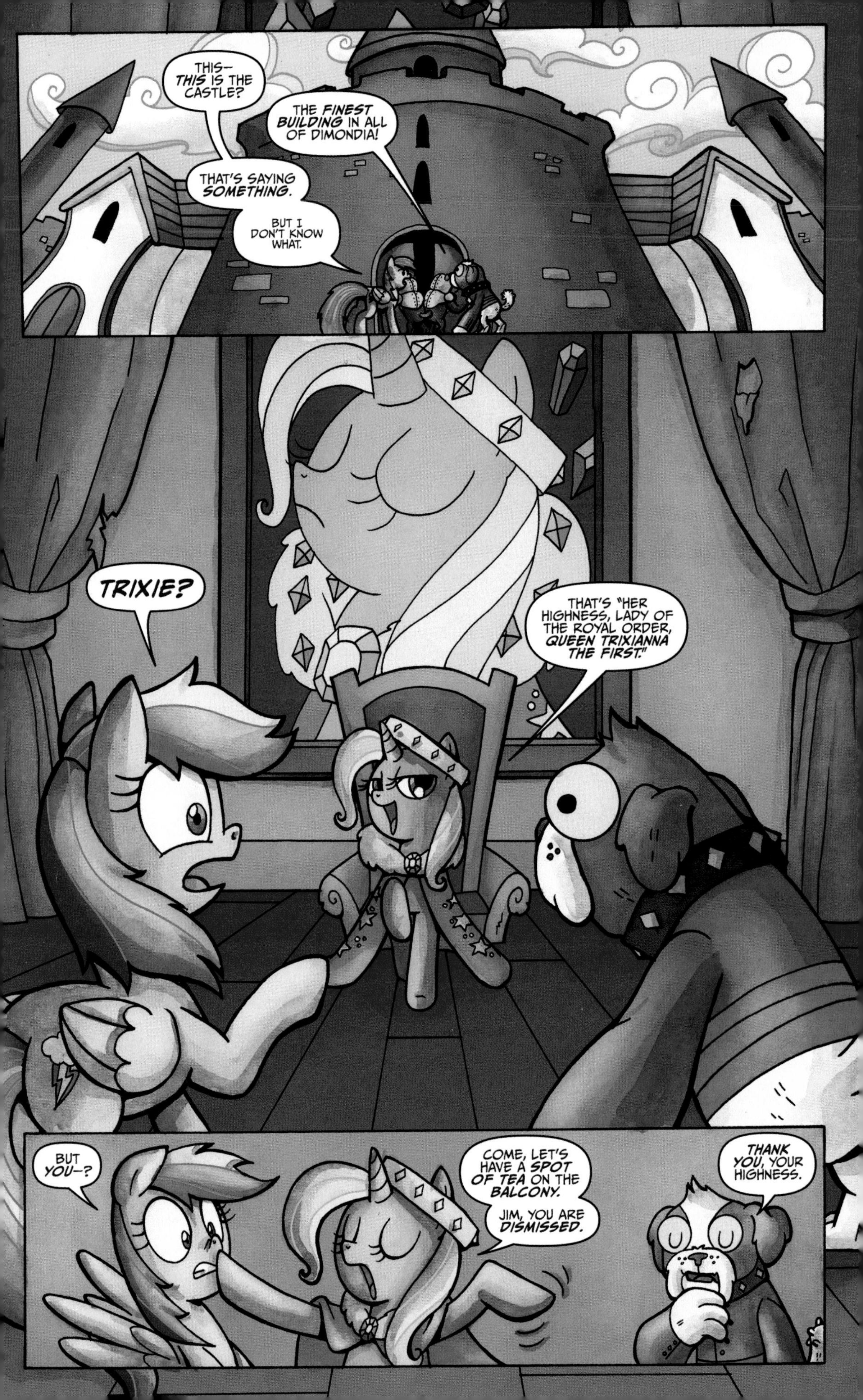
THIS— THIS IS THE CASTLE?
THE FINEST BUILDING IN ALL OF DIMONDIA!
THAT'S SAYING SOMETHING.
BUT I DON'T KNOW WHAT.
TRIXIE?
THAT'S "HER HIGHNESS, LADY OF THE ROYAL ORDER, QUEEN TRIXIANNA THE FIRST."
BUT YOU–?
COME, LET'S HAVE A SPOT OF TEA ON THE BALCONY.
JIM, YOU ARE DISMISSED.
THANK YOU, YOUR HIGHNESS.

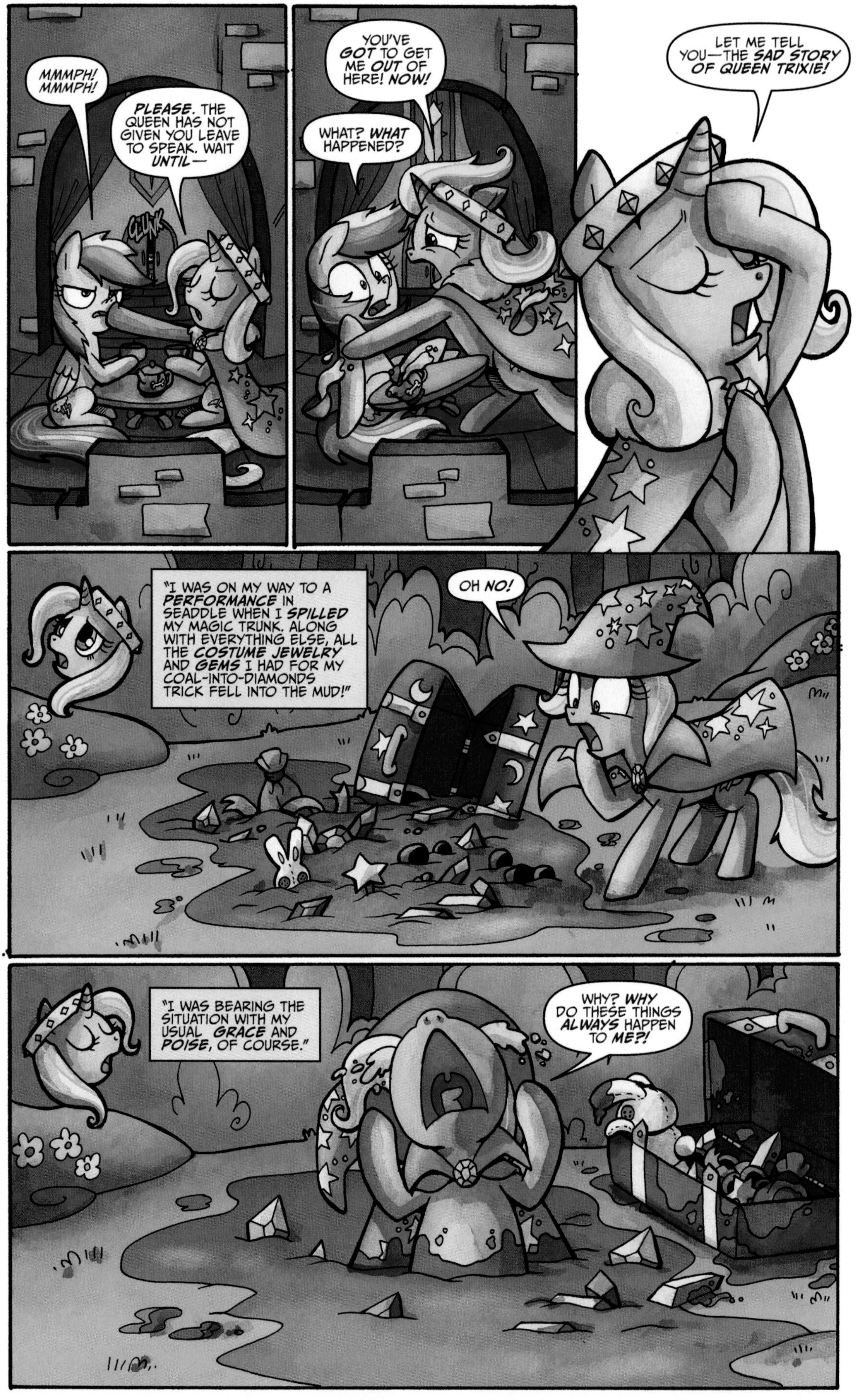
MMMPH! MMMPH!
PLEASE. THE QUEEN HAS NOT GIVEN YOU LEAVE TO SPEAK. WAIT UNTIL—
CLUNK
YOU'VE GOT TO GET ME OUT OF HERE! NOW!
WHAT? WHAT HAPPENED?
LET ME TELL YOU—THE SAD STORY OF QUEEN TRIXIE!
"I WAS ON MY WAY TO A PERFORMANCE IN SEADDLE WHEN I SPILLED MY MAGIC TRUNK. ALONG WITH EVERYTHING ELSE, ALL THE COSTUME JEWELRY AND GEMS I HAD FOR MY COAL-INTO-DIAMONDS TRICK FELL INTO THE MUD!"
OH NO!
"I WAS BEARING THE SITUATION WITH MY USUAL GRACE AND POISE, OF COURSE."
WHY? WHY DO THESE THINGS ALWAYS HAPPEN TO ME?!

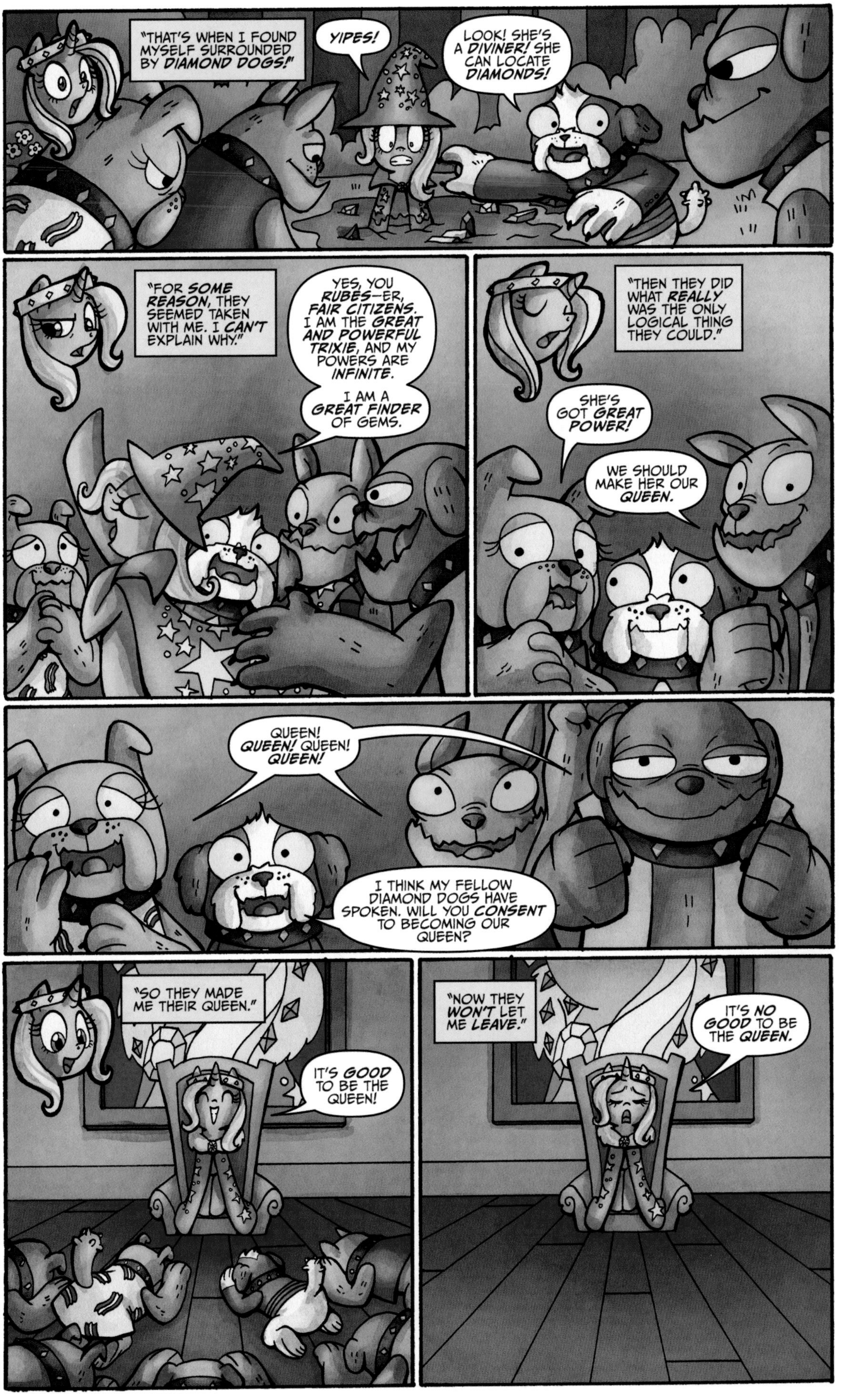
"THAT'S WHEN I FOUND MYSELF SURROUNDED BY DIAMOND DOGS!"
YIPES!
LOOK! SHE'S A DIVINER! SHE CAN LOCATE DIAMONDS!
"FOR SOME REASON, THEY SEEMED TAKEN WITH ME. I CAN'T EXPLAIN WHY."
YES, YOU RUBES—ER, FAIR CITIZENS. I AM THE GREAT AND POWERFUL TRIXIE, AND MY POWERS ARE INFINITE.
I AM A GREAT FINDER OF GEMS.
"THEN THEY DID WHAT REALLY WAS THE ONLY LOGICAL THING THEY COULD."
SHE'S GOT GREAT POWER!
WE SHOULD MAKE HER OUR QUEEN.
QUEEN! QUEEN! QUEEN! QUEEN!
I THINK MY FELLOW DIAMOND DOGS HAVE SPOKEN. WILL YOU CONSENT TO BECOMING OUR QUEEN?
"SO THEY MADE ME THEIR QUEEN."
IT'S GOOD TO BE THE QUEEN!
"NOW THEY WON'T LET ME LEAVE."
IT'S NO GOOD TO BE THE QUEEN.

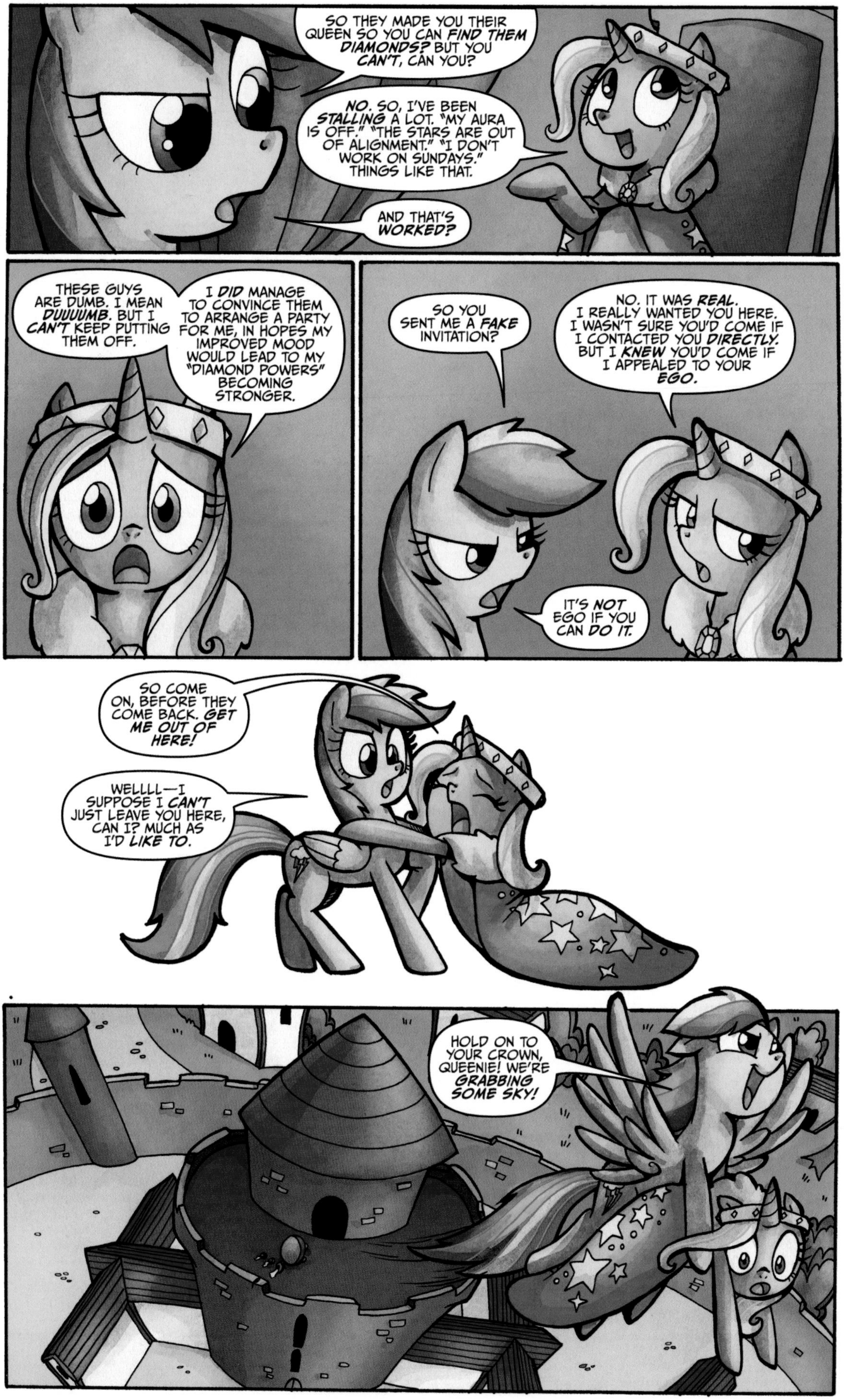
SO THEY MADE YOU THEIR QUEEN SO YOU CAN *FIND THEM DIAMONDS?* BUT YOU *CAN'T*, CAN YOU?
NO. SO, I'VE BEEN *STALLING* A LOT. "MY AURA IS OFF." "THE STARS ARE OUT OF ALIGNMENT." "I DON'T WORK ON SUNDAYS." THINGS LIKE THAT.
AND THAT'S *WORKED?*
THESE GUYS ARE DUMB. I MEAN *DUUUUMB*. BUT I *CAN'T* KEEP PUTTING THEM OFF.
I *DID* MANAGE TO CONVINCE THEM TO ARRANGE A PARTY FOR ME, IN HOPES MY IMPROVED MOOD WOULD LEAD TO MY "DIAMOND POWERS" BECOMING STRONGER.
SO YOU SENT ME A *FAKE* INVITATION?
NO. IT WAS *REAL*. I REALLY WANTED YOU HERE. I WASN'T SURE YOU'D COME IF I CONTACTED YOU *DIRECTLY*. BUT I *KNEW* YOU'D COME IF I APPEALED TO YOUR *EGO*.
IT'S *NOT* EGO IF YOU CAN *DO IT*.
SO COME ON, BEFORE THEY COME BACK. *GET ME OUT OF HERE!*
WELLLL—I SUPPOSE I *CAN'T* JUST LEAVE YOU HERE, CAN I? MUCH AS I'D *LIKE TO*.
HOLD ON TO YOUR CROWN, QUEENIE! WE'RE *GRABBING SOME SKY!*

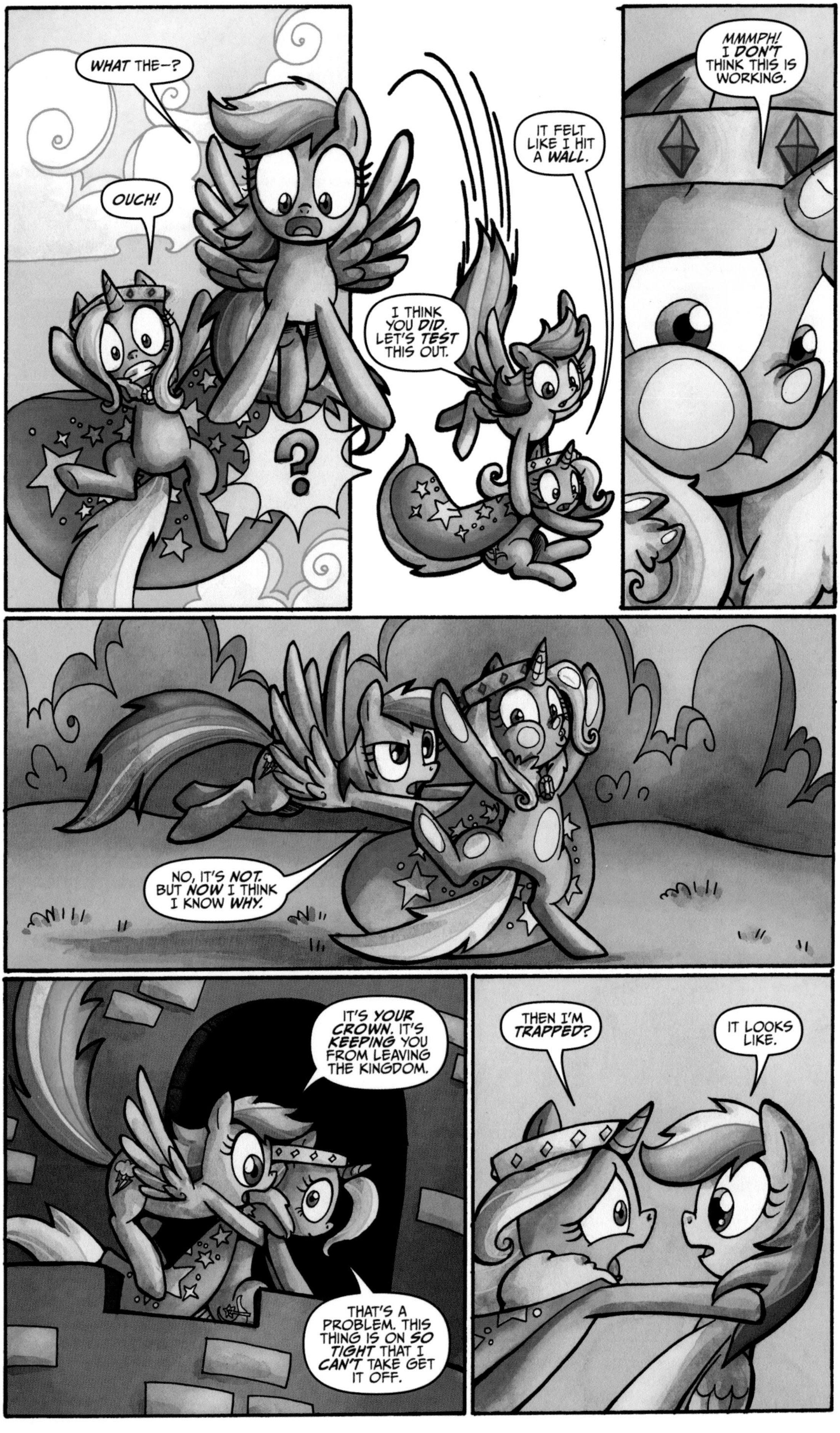
WHAT THE–?
OUCH!
IT FELT LIKE I HIT A WALL.
I THINK YOU DID. LET'S TEST THIS OUT.
MMMPH! I DON'T THINK THIS IS WORKING.
NO, IT'S NOT. BUT NOW I THINK I KNOW WHY.
IT'S YOUR CROWN. IT'S KEEPING YOU FROM LEAVING THE KINGDOM.
THAT'S A PROBLEM. THIS THING IS ON SO TIGHT THAT I CAN'T TAKE GET IT OFF.
THEN I'M TRAPPED?
IT LOOKS LIKE.

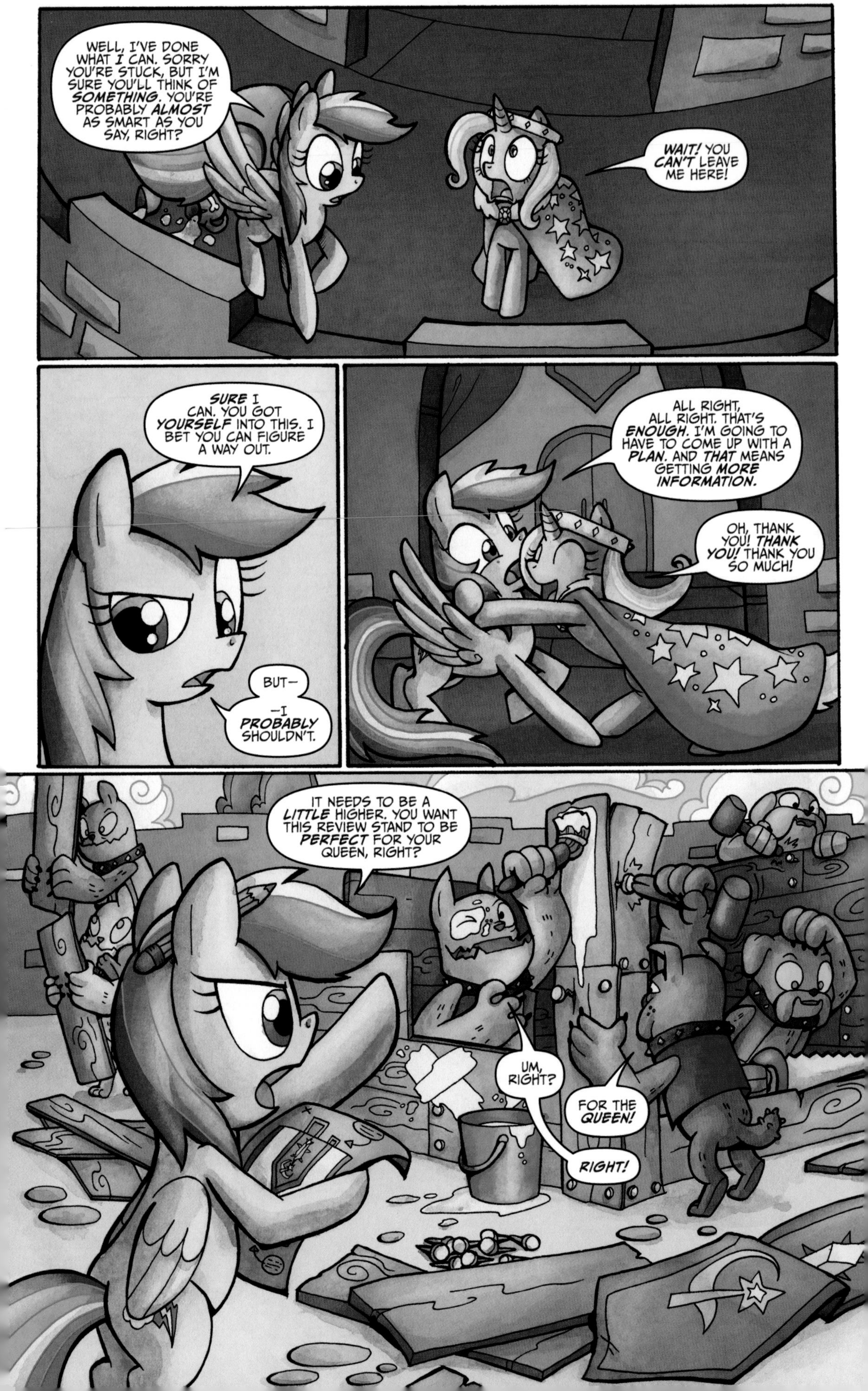
WELL, I'VE DONE WHAT I CAN. SORRY YOU'RE STUCK, BUT I'M SURE YOU'LL THINK OF SOMETHING. YOU'RE PROBABLY ALMOST AS SMART AS YOU SAY, RIGHT?
WAIT! YOU CAN'T LEAVE ME HERE!
SURE I CAN. YOU GOT YOURSELF INTO THIS. I BET YOU CAN FIGURE A WAY OUT.
BUT—
—I PROBABLY SHOULDN'T.
ALL RIGHT, ALL RIGHT. THAT'S ENOUGH. I'M GOING TO HAVE TO COME UP WITH A PLAN. AND THAT MEANS GETTING MORE INFORMATION.
OH, THANK YOU! THANK YOU! THANK YOU SO MUCH!
IT NEEDS TO BE A LITTLE HIGHER. YOU WANT THIS REVIEW STAND TO BE PERFECT FOR YOUR QUEEN, RIGHT?
UM, RIGHT?
FOR THE QUEEN!
RIGHT!

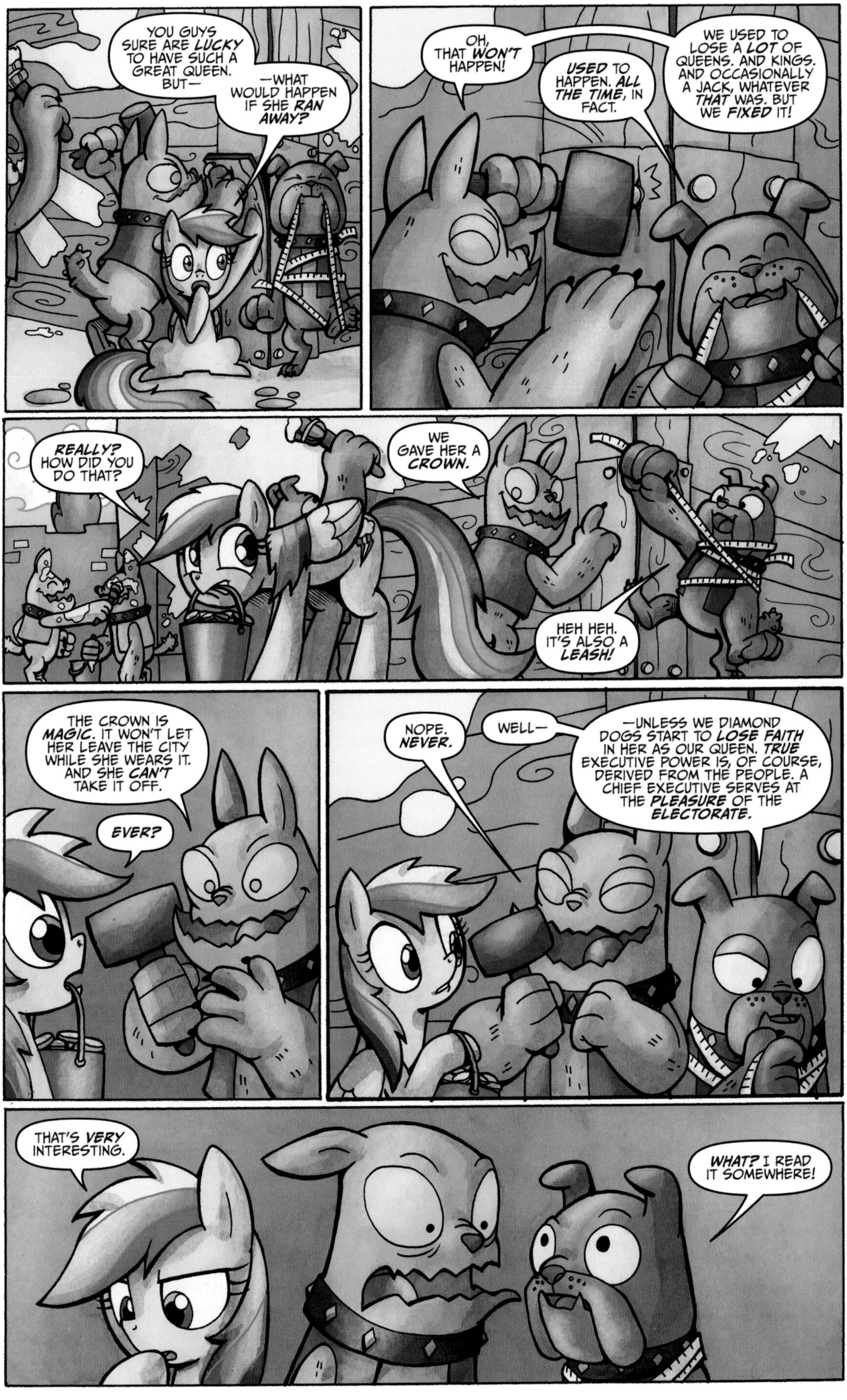
YOU GUYS SURE ARE LUCKY TO HAVE SUCH A GREAT QUEEN. BUT—
—WHAT WOULD HAPPEN IF SHE RAN AWAY?
OH, THAT WON'T HAPPEN!
USED TO HAPPEN. ALL THE TIME, IN FACT.
WE USED TO LOSE A LOT OF QUEENS. AND KINGS. AND OCCASIONALLY A JACK, WHATEVER THAT WAS. BUT WE FIXED IT!
REALLY? HOW DID YOU DO THAT?
WE GAVE HER A CROWN.
HEH HEH. IT'S ALSO A LEASH!
THE CROWN IS MAGIC. IT WON'T LET HER LEAVE THE CITY WHILE SHE WEARS IT. AND SHE CAN'T TAKE IT OFF.
EVER?
NOPE. NEVER.
WELL—
—UNLESS WE DIAMOND DOGS START TO LOSE FAITH IN HER AS OUR QUEEN. TRUE EXECUTIVE POWER IS, OF COURSE, DERIVED FROM THE PEOPLE. A CHIEF EXECUTIVE SERVES AT THE PLEASURE OF THE ELECTORATE.
THAT'S VERY INTERESTING.
WHAT? I READ IT SOMEWHERE!

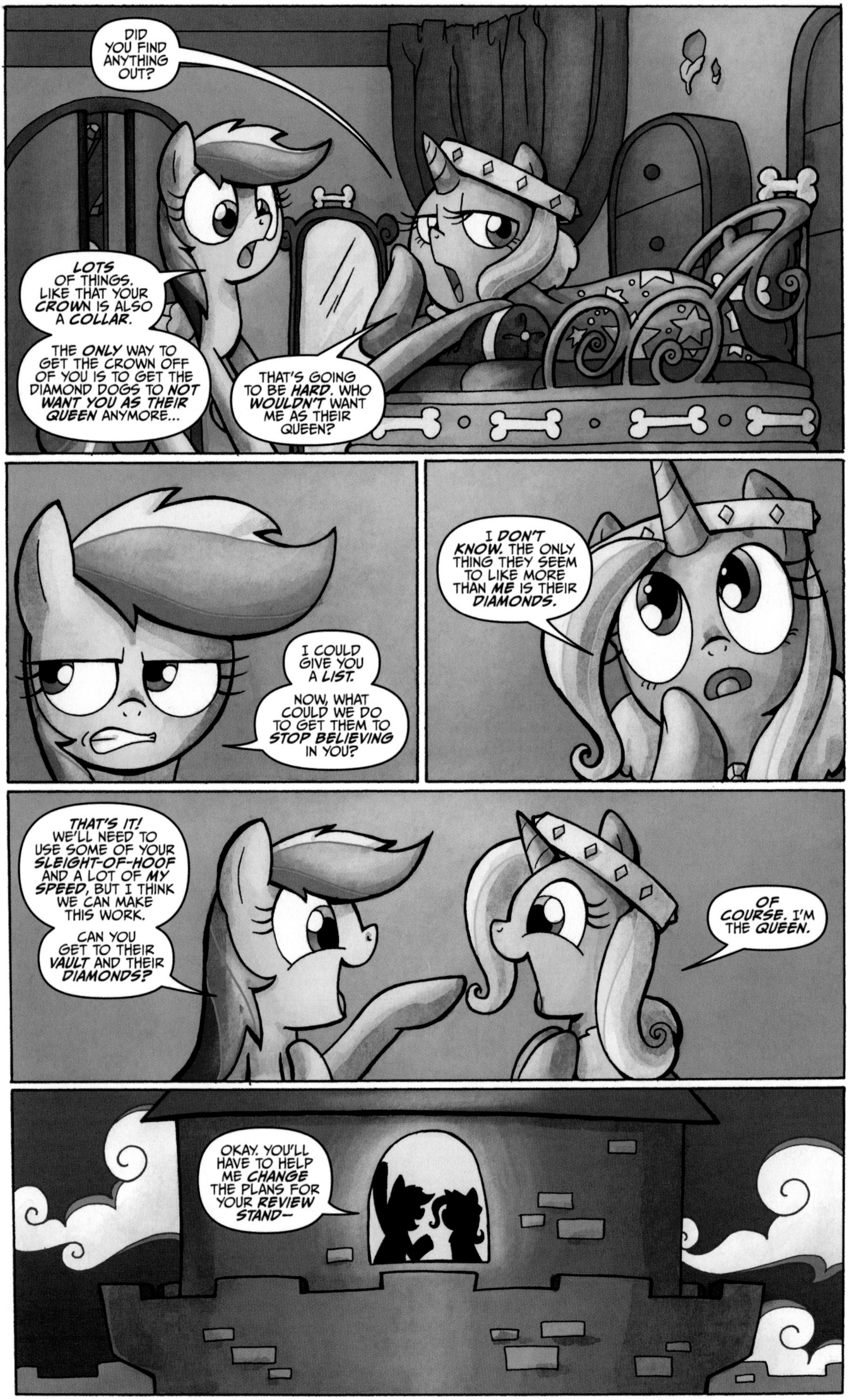
DID YOU FIND ANYTHING OUT?
LOTS OF THINGS. LIKE THAT YOUR CROWN IS ALSO A COLLAR.
THE ONLY WAY TO GET THE CROWN OFF OF YOU IS TO GET THE DIAMOND DOGS TO NOT WANT YOU AS THEIR QUEEN ANYMORE...
THAT'S GOING TO BE HARD. WHO WOULDN'T WANT ME AS THEIR QUEEN?
I COULD GIVE YOU A LIST.
NOW, WHAT COULD WE DO TO GET THEM TO STOP BELIEVING IN YOU?
I DON'T KNOW. THE ONLY THING THEY SEEM TO LIKE MORE THAN ME IS THEIR DIAMONDS.
THAT'S IT! WE'LL NEED TO USE SOME OF YOUR SLEIGHT-OF-HOOF AND A LOT OF MY SPEED, BUT I THINK WE CAN MAKE THIS WORK.
CAN YOU GET TO THEIR VAULT AND THEIR DIAMONDS?
OF COURSE. I'M THE QUEEN.
OKAY. YOU'LL HAVE TO HELP ME CHANGE THE PLANS FOR YOUR REVIEW STAND—

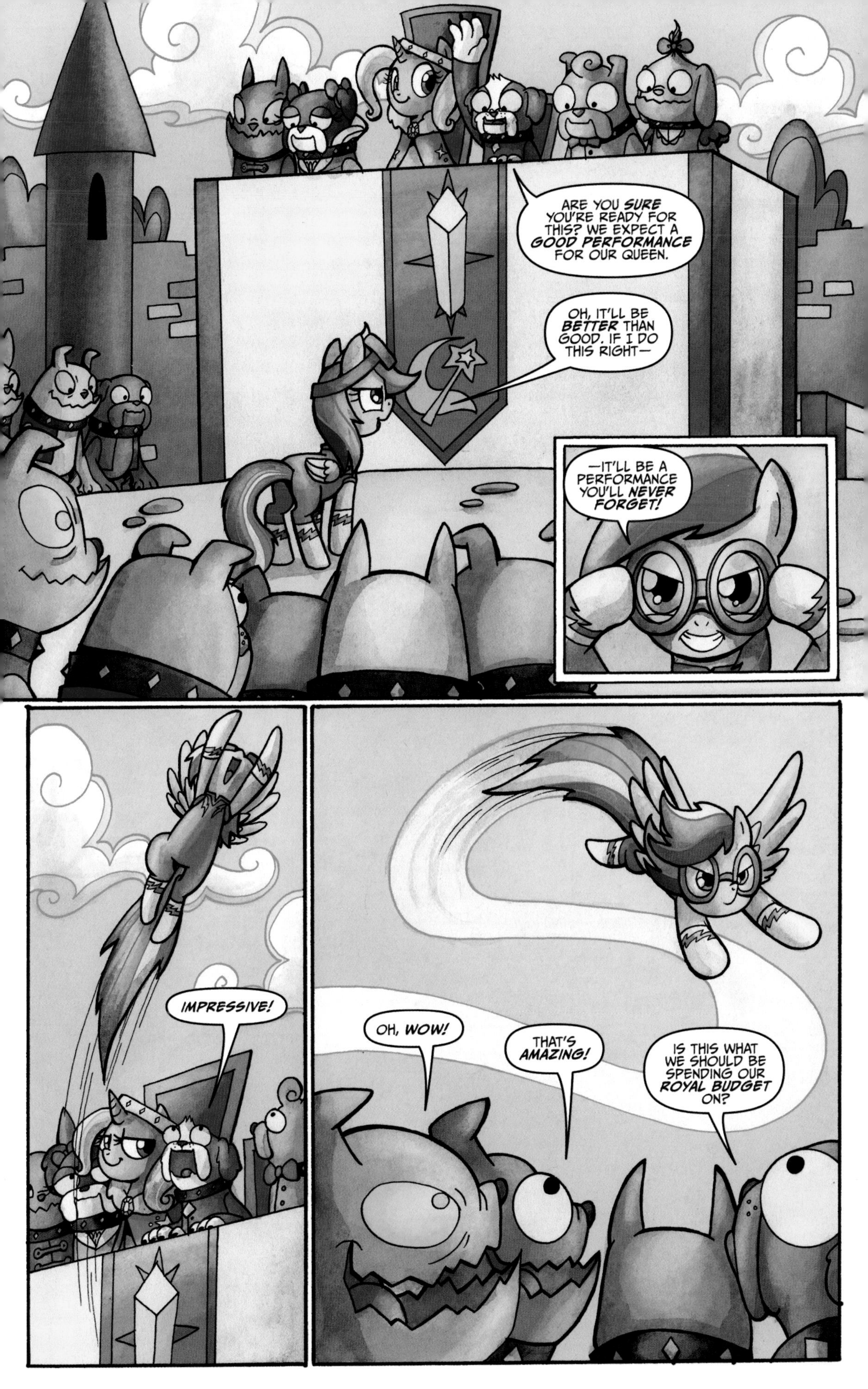
ARE YOU SURE YOU'RE READY FOR THIS? WE EXPECT A GOOD PERFORMANCE FOR OUR QUEEN.
OH, IT'LL BE BETTER THAN GOOD. IF I DO THIS RIGHT—
—IT'LL BE A PERFORMANCE YOU'LL NEVER FORGET!
IMPRESSIVE!
OH, WOW!
THAT'S AMAZING!
IS THIS WHAT WE SHOULD BE SPENDING OUR ROYAL BUDGET ON?

SHE IS *FANTASTIC*, MY QUEEN!

YES, *INDEED*. I'VE NEVER SEEN *ANYTHING* LIKE THIS.

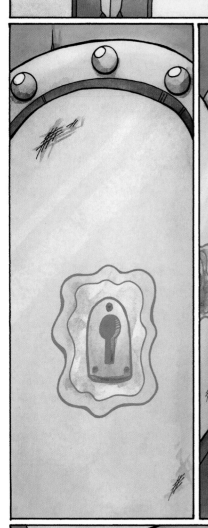

OH MY! THAT LOOKS *HARD*.

YOU HAVE *NO IDEA*.

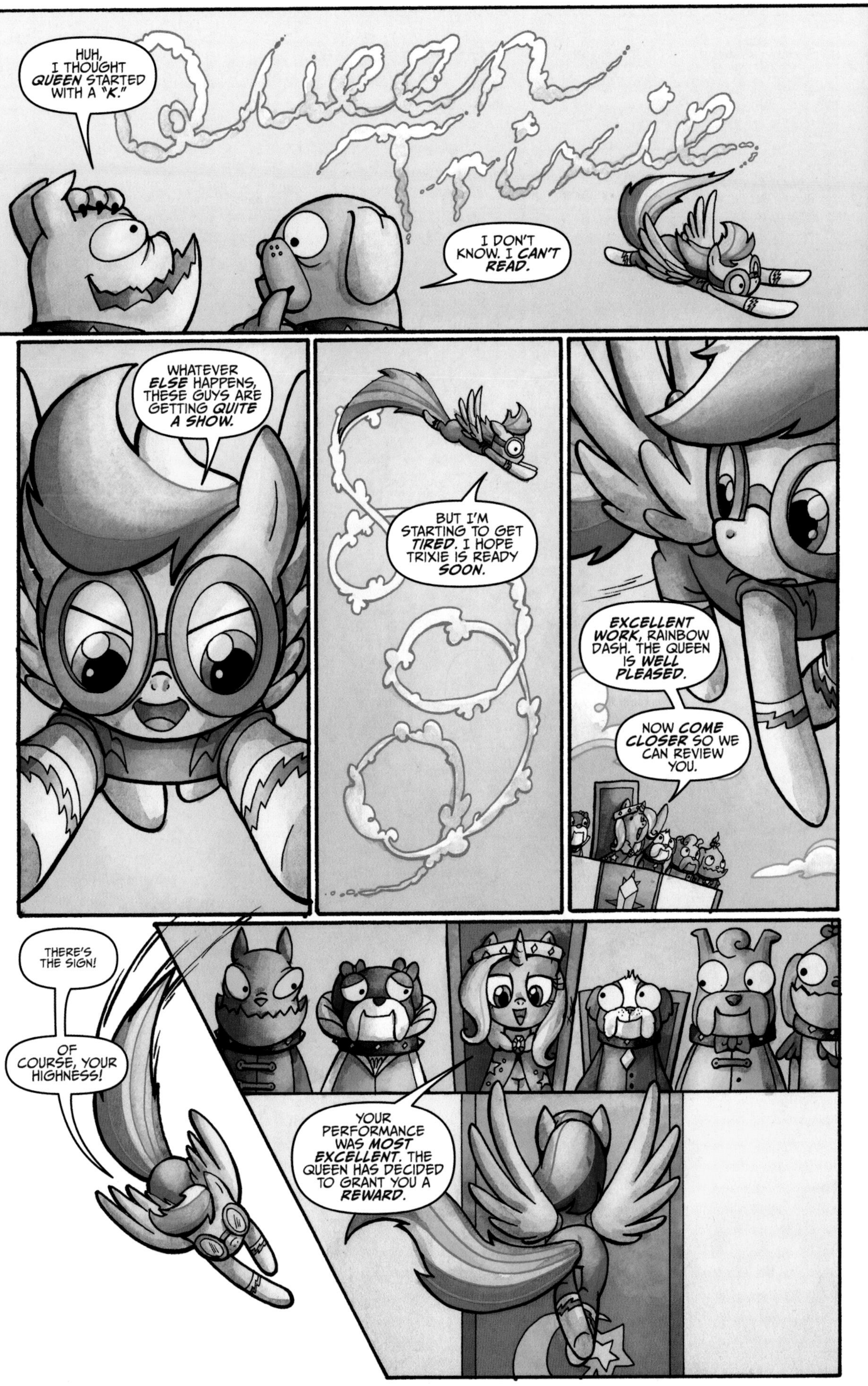
Queen Trixie
HUH, I THOUGHT QUEEN STARTED WITH A "K."
I DON'T KNOW. I CAN'T READ.
WHATEVER ELSE HAPPENS, THESE GUYS ARE GETTING QUITE A SHOW.
BUT I'M STARTING TO GET TIRED. I HOPE TRIXIE IS READY SOON.
EXCELLENT WORK, RAINBOW DASH. THE QUEEN IS WELL PLEASED.
NOW COME CLOSER SO WE CAN REVIEW YOU.
THERE'S THE SIGN!
OF COURSE, YOUR HIGHNESS!
YOUR PERFORMANCE WAS MOST EXCELLENT. THE QUEEN HAS DECIDED TO GRANT YOU A REWARD.

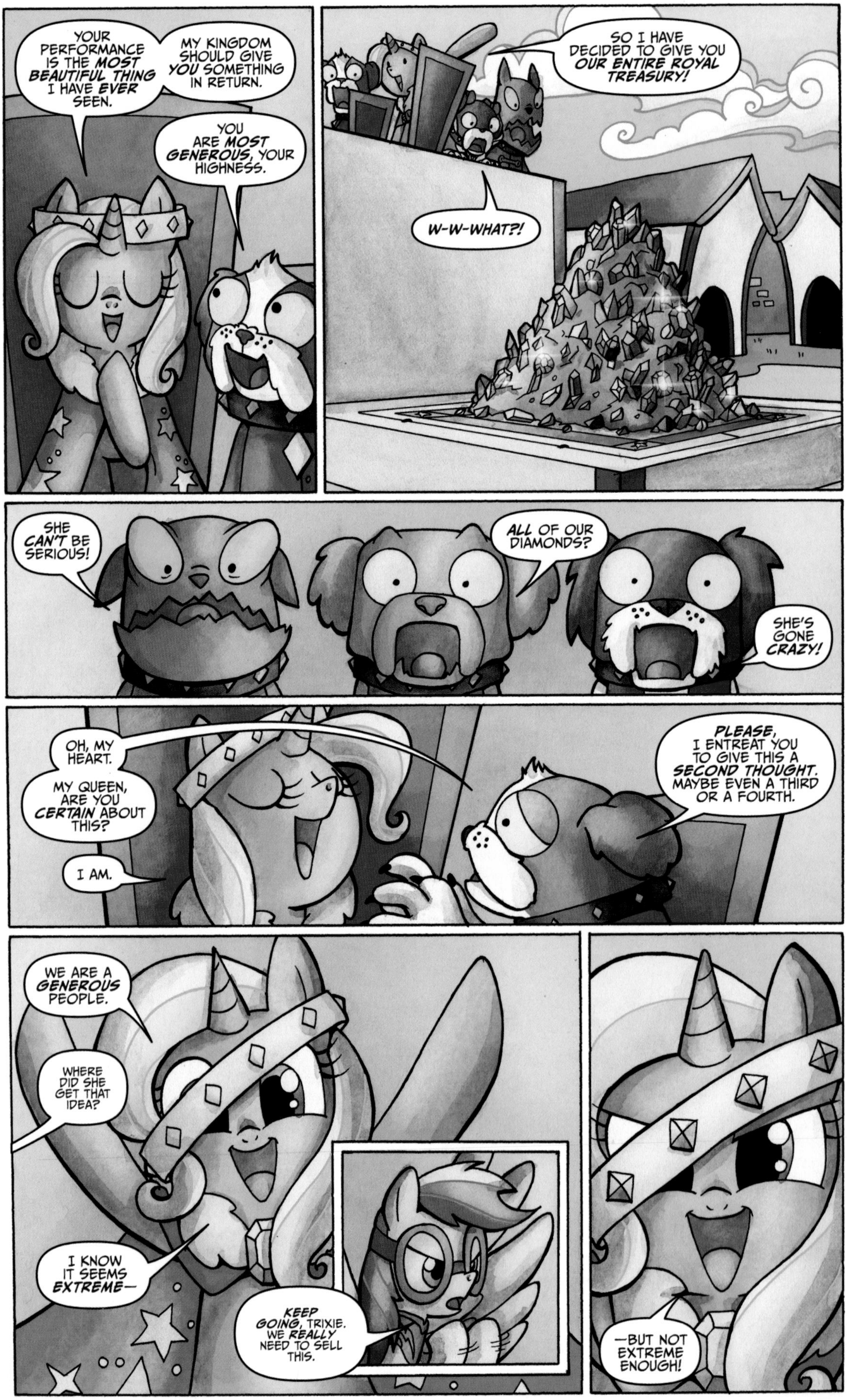
YOUR PERFORMANCE IS THE MOST BEAUTIFUL THING I HAVE EVER SEEN.
MY KINGDOM SHOULD GIVE YOU SOMETHING IN RETURN.
YOU ARE MOST GENEROUS, YOUR HIGHNESS.
SO I HAVE DECIDED TO GIVE YOU OUR ENTIRE ROYAL TREASURY!
W-W-WHAT?!
SHE CAN'T BE SERIOUS!
ALL OF OUR DIAMONDS?
SHE'S GONE CRAZY!
OH, MY HEART.
MY QUEEN, ARE YOU CERTAIN ABOUT THIS?
I AM.
PLEASE, I ENTREAT YOU TO GIVE THIS A SECOND THOUGHT. MAYBE EVEN A THIRD OR A FOURTH.
WE ARE A GENEROUS PEOPLE.
WHERE DID SHE GET THAT IDEA?
I KNOW IT SEEMS EXTREME—
KEEP GOING, TRIXIE. WE REALLY NEED TO SELL THIS.
—BUT NOT EXTREME ENOUGH!

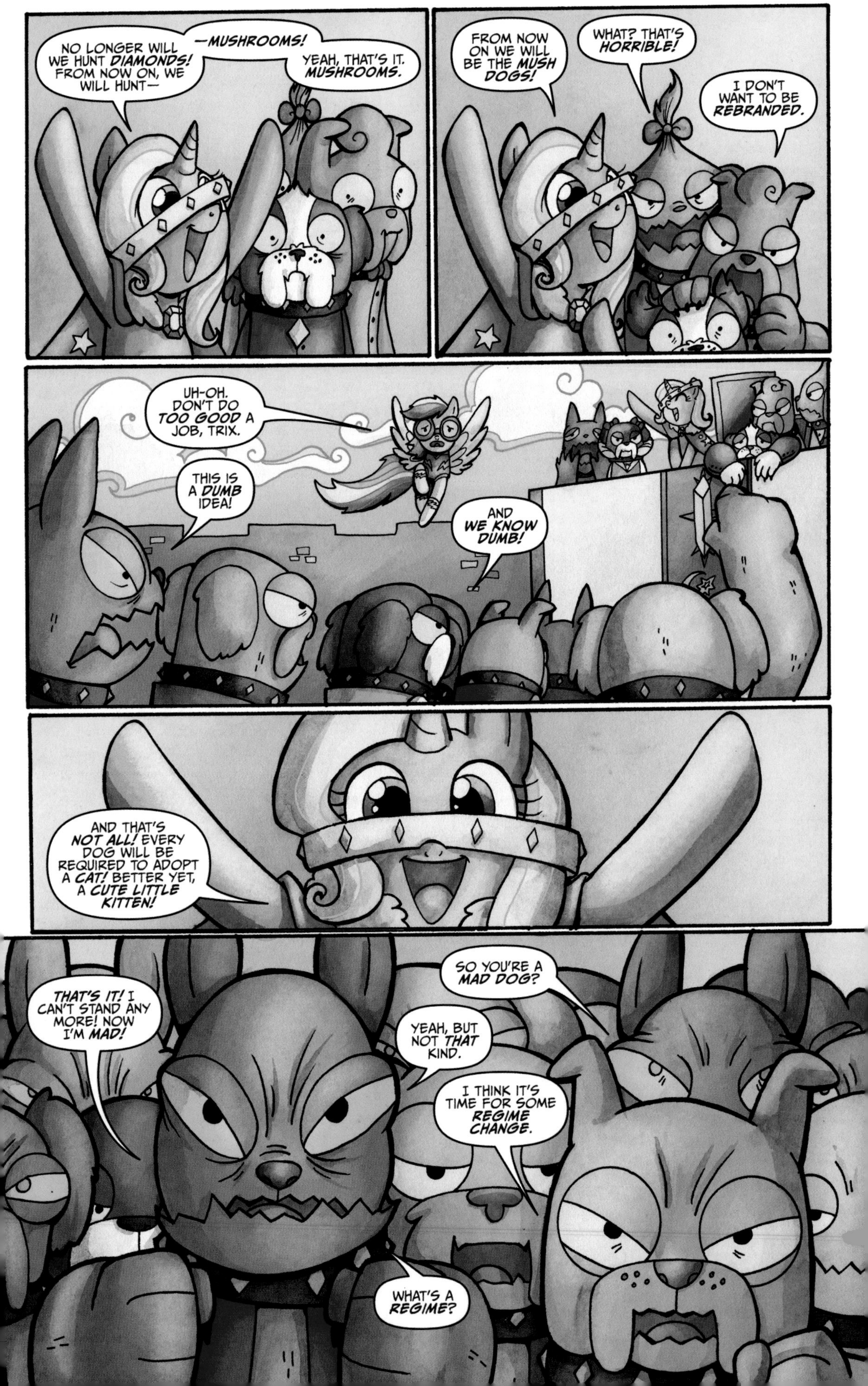

NO LONGER WILL WE HUNT *DIAMONDS!* FROM NOW ON, WE WILL HUNT—
—*MUSHROOMS!*
YEAH, THAT'S IT. *MUSHROOMS.*
FROM NOW ON WE WILL BE THE *MUSH DOGS!*
WHAT? THAT'S *HORRIBLE!*
I DON'T WANT TO BE *REBRANDED.*
UH-OH. DON'T DO *TOO GOOD* A JOB, TRIX.
THIS IS A *DUMB* IDEA!
AND *WE KNOW DUMB!*
AND THAT'S *NOT ALL!* EVERY DOG WILL BE REQUIRED TO ADOPT A *CAT!* BETTER YET, A *CUTE LITTLE KITTEN!*
THAT'S IT! I CAN'T STAND ANY MORE! NOW I'M *MAD!*
SO YOU'RE A *MAD DOG?*
YEAH, BUT NOT *THAT* KIND.
I THINK IT'S TIME FOR SOME *REGIME CHANGE.*
WHAT'S A *REGIME?*

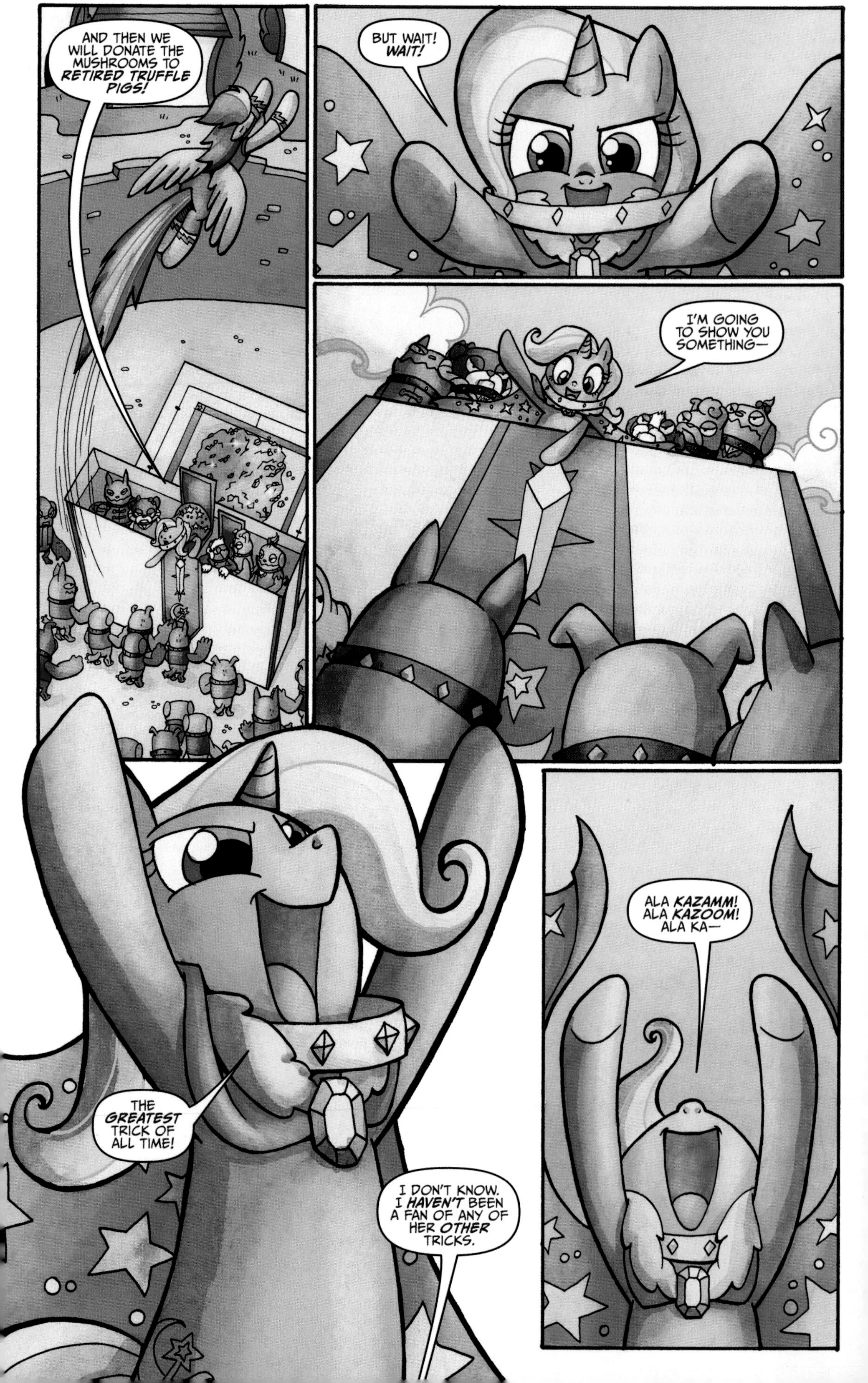
AND THEN WE WILL DONATE THE MUSHROOMS TO *RETIRED TRUFFLE PIGS!*
BUT WAIT! *WAIT!*
I'M GOING TO SHOW YOU SOMETHING—
THE *GREATEST* TRICK OF ALL TIME!
I DON'T KNOW. I *HAVEN'T* BEEN A FAN OF ANY OF HER *OTHER* TRICKS.
ALA *KAZAMM!* ALA *KAZOOM!* ALA KA—

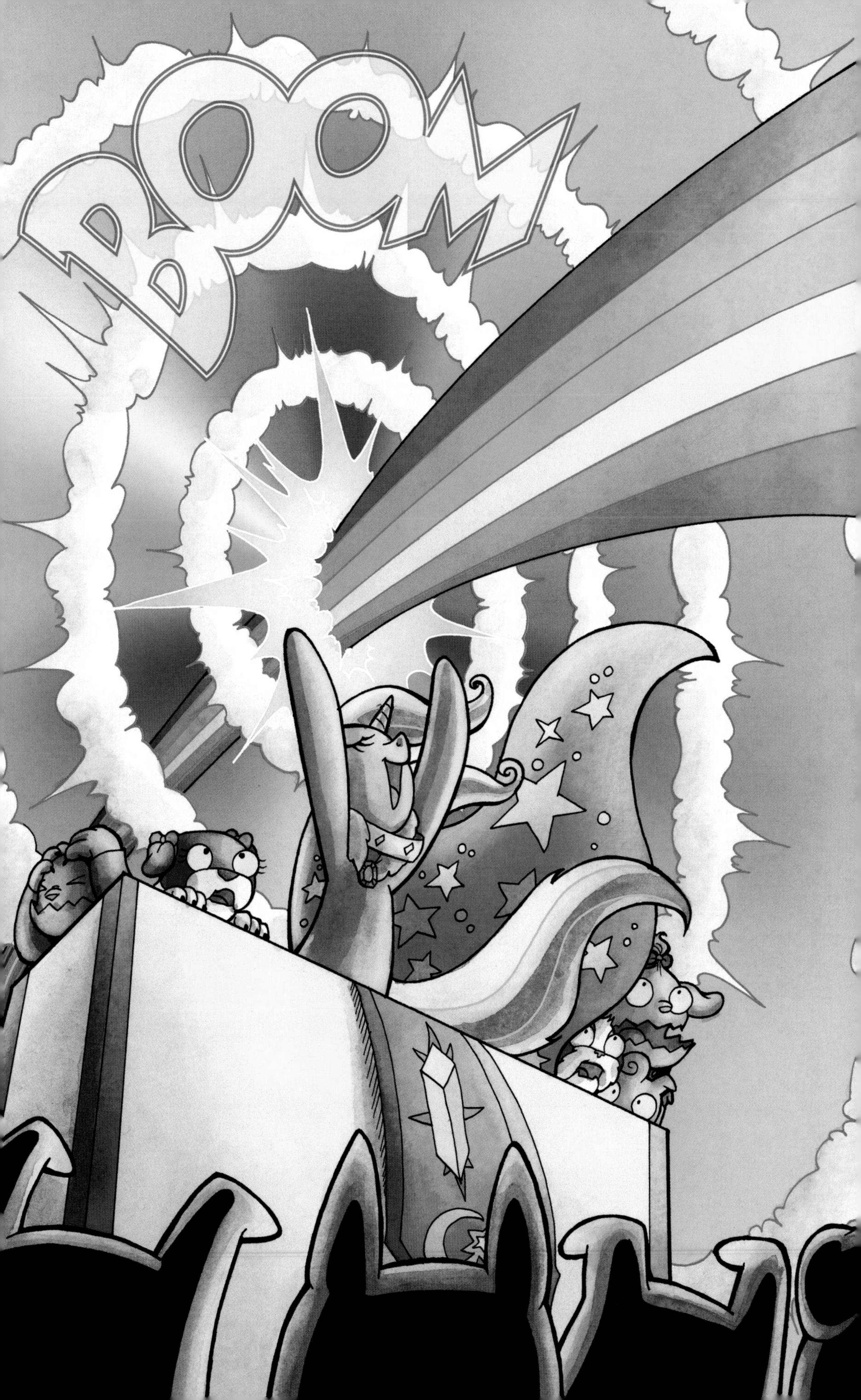
BOOM

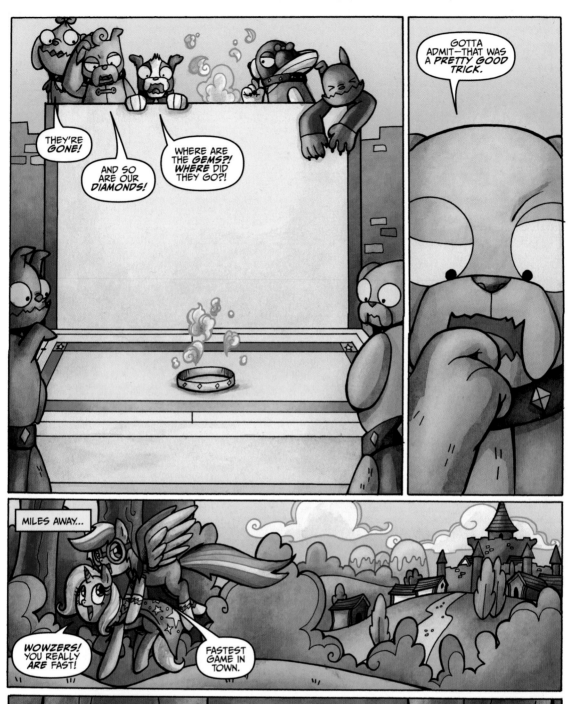

THEY'RE GONE!

AND SO ARE OUR DIAMONDS!

WHERE ARE THE GEMS?! WHERE DID THEY GO?!

GOTTA ADMIT—THAT WAS A PRETTY GOOD TRICK.

MILES AWAY...

WOWZERS! YOU REALLY ARE FAST!

FASTEST GAME IN TOWN.

SO—

—YOU THINK THEY'LL EVER FIND THEIR DIAMONDS?

PROBABLY. THEY'RE NOT THAT DUMB.

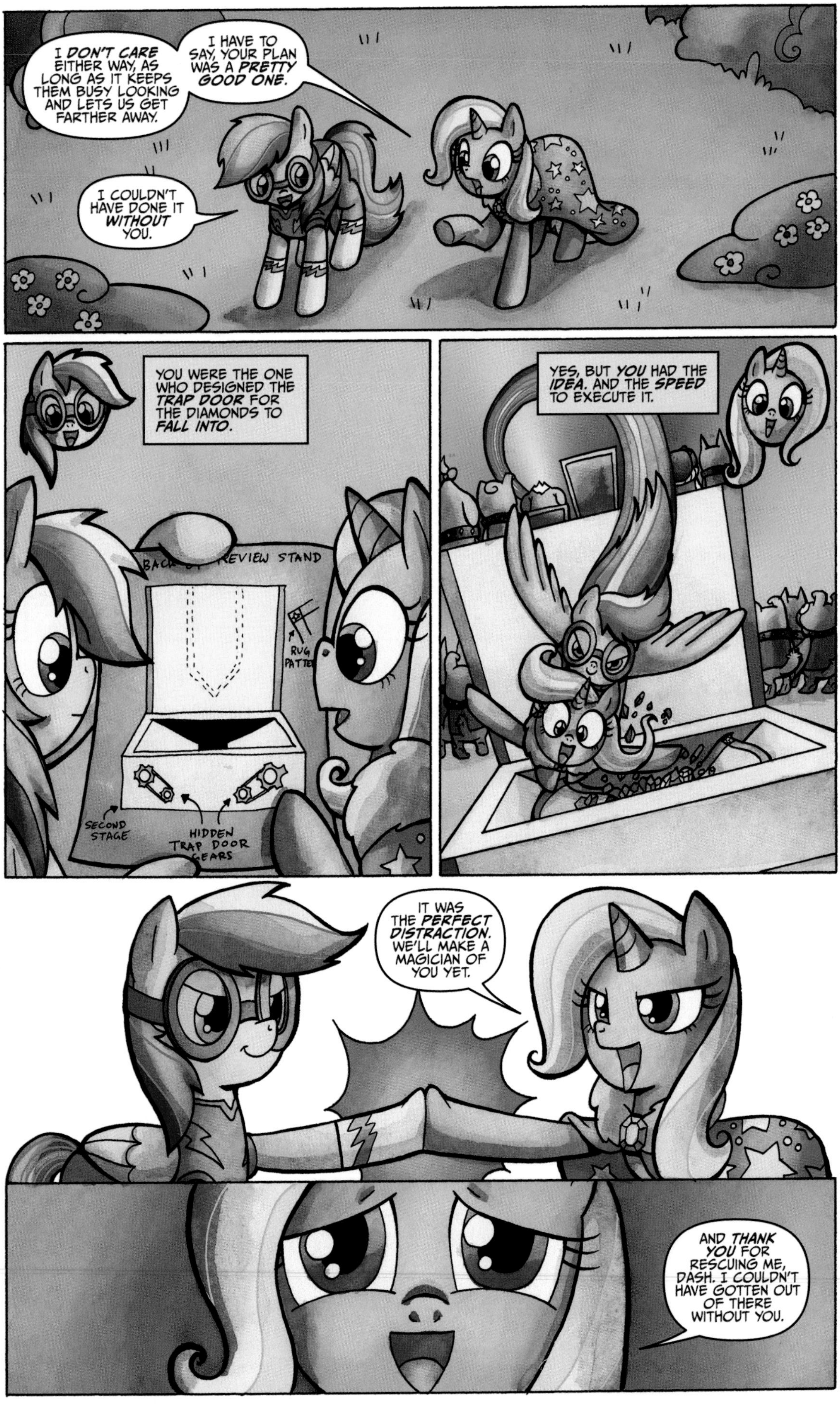
I DON'T CARE EITHER WAY, AS LONG AS IT KEEPS THEM BUSY LOOKING AND LETS US GET FARTHER AWAY.
I HAVE TO SAY, YOUR PLAN WAS A PRETTY GOOD ONE.
I COULDN'T HAVE DONE IT WITHOUT YOU.
YOU WERE THE ONE WHO DESIGNED THE TRAP DOOR FOR THE DIAMONDS TO FALL INTO.
REVIEW STAND
RUG
SECOND STAGE
HIDDEN TRAP DOOR GEARS
YES, BUT YOU HAD THE IDEA. AND THE SPEED TO EXECUTE IT.
IT WAS THE PERFECT DISTRACTION. WE'LL MAKE A MAGICIAN OF YOU YET.
AND THANK YOU FOR RESCUING ME, DASH. I COULDN'T HAVE GOTTEN OUT OF THERE WITHOUT YOU.

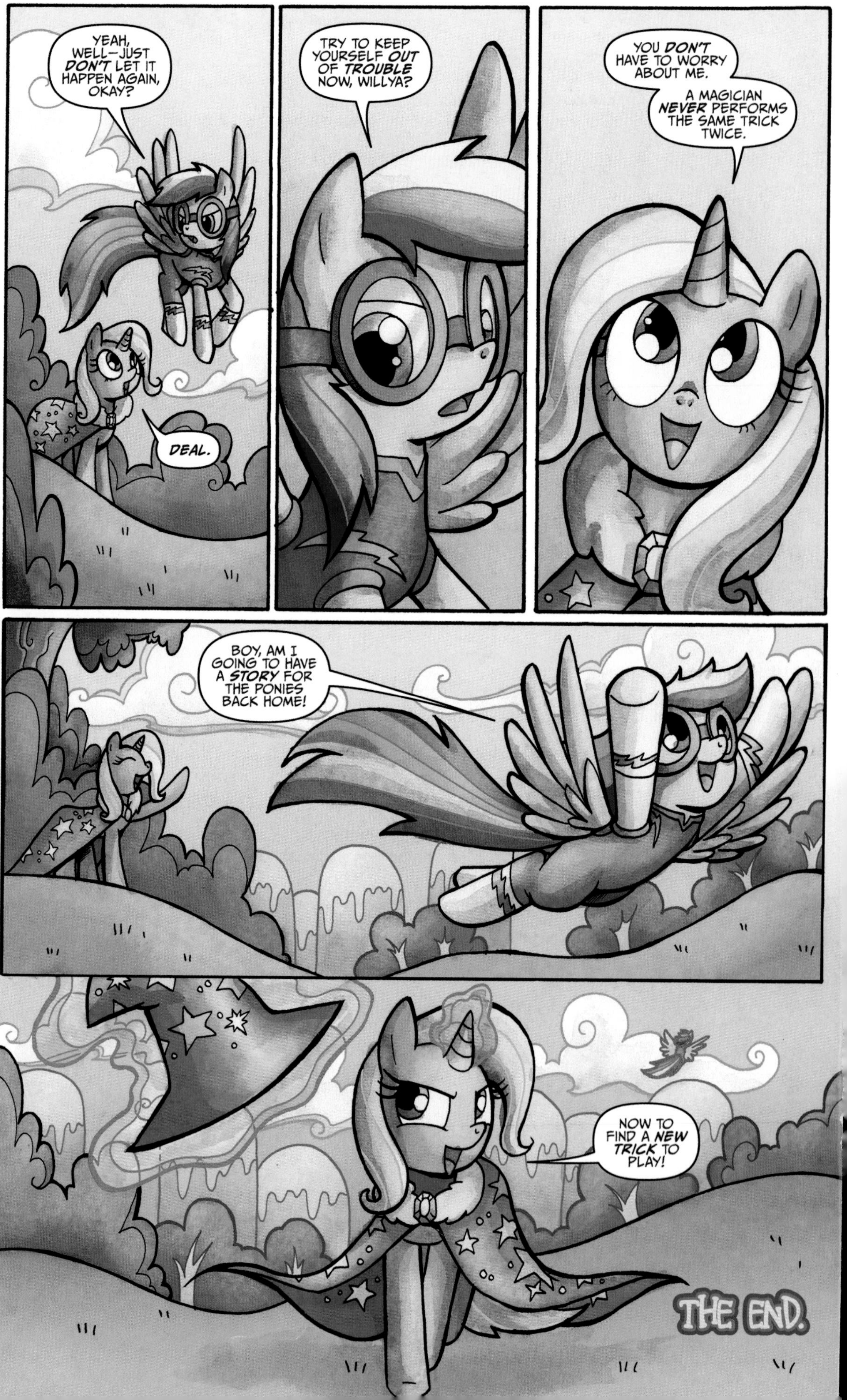
YEAH, WELL—JUST DON'T LET IT HAPPEN AGAIN, OKAY?
DEAL.
TRY TO KEEP YOURSELF OUT OF TROUBLE NOW, WILLYA?
YOU DON'T HAVE TO WORRY ABOUT ME.
A MAGICIAN NEVER PERFORMS THE SAME TRICK TWICE.
BOY, AM I GOING TO HAVE A STORY FOR THE PONIES BACK HOME!
NOW TO FIND A NEW TRICK TO PLAY!
THE END.